Sleds on Boston Common

Margaret K. McElderry Books
An imprint of Simon & Schuster
Children's Publishing Division
1230 Avenue of the Americas
New York, New York 10020

Text copyright © 2000 by Louise Borden
Illustrations copyright © 2000 by
Robert Andrew Parker

Book design by Ann Bobco.
The text of this book was set in Centaur MT.
The illustrations were rendered in watercolor.

Printed in Hong Kong

10 9 8 7 6 5 4 3

Library of Congress Cataloging-in-Publication Data
Borden, Louise.
Sleds on Boston Common : a story from the
American Revolution / by Louise Borden ;
illustrated by Robert Andrew Parker.
p. cm.
Summary: Henry complains to the royal governor,
General Gage, after his plan to sled down the steep
hill at Boston Common is thwarted by the masses
of British troops camped there.
ISBN: 0-689-82812-8
I. Boston (Mass.)—History—Colonial period, ca.
1600-1775—Juvenile fiction. 2. Gage, Thomas,
1721-1787—Juvenile fiction. [I. Boston
(Mass.)—History—Colonial period, ca. 1600-
1775—Fiction. 2. Gage, Thomas, 1721-1787—
Fiction.] I. Parker, Robert Andrew, ill. II. Title.
PZ7.B64827Gg 2000 [E]—dc21 99-18080

Sleds
on
Boston Common

A Story from the American Revolution

written by
LOUISE BORDEN

illustrated by
ROBERT ANDREW PARKER

MARGARET K. McELDERRY BOOKS

———————————— O ————————————

*I*n December of 1774,
times were hard for all of us in Boston.
Few good folk had coins to spare
when they walked past the window
of my father's shop on King Street . . .
the best place to buy English and Dutch toys,
spectacles,
flutes,
or the maps that my father drew with his own hand.

Sometimes he let me color the maps
with his paints and his pens.
"In a few years, Henry,
your steady hand will be better than mine."
That's what my father, William Price, said.

---○---

Months ago, on the first day of June,
the British closed our harbor
𝔅𝔶 𝔬𝔯𝔡𝔢𝔯 𝔬𝔣 𝔱𝔥𝔢 𝔎𝔦𝔫𝔤 𝔬𝔣 𝔈𝔫𝔤𝔩𝔞𝔫𝔡, 𝔊𝔢𝔬𝔯𝔤𝔢 III.
King George wanted to punish those in Boston
who spoke against his laws
that were made across the sea:
patriots like Sam Adams
and John Hancock
and other town leaders . . .
and patriots like my father
and my friends' fathers . . .
All over Boston, south and north,
people were not happy with King George III.

Or with our new royal governor, General Thomas Gage.
General Gage was King George's top general,
the commander of every British soldier in North America.
Since May,
he had lived in one of the biggest,
tallest houses in all of Boston.
Whenever my brothers and I walked to school,
we passed by the redbrick front of Province House.
I always looked up at the weather vane high on the cupola:
a gold Indian archer that shone in the sun.
Thomas Gage was a powerful man indeed.

On the day he closed our harbor,
church bells rang in every colony in America.
Other patriots in other towns said:
"We will stand beside Boston in these hard times.
We are all Americans together."

o　o　o

Now only the king's ships could enter or leave our harbor.
And so there was no trade.
There was little work for the men on Long Wharf,
once the busiest dock in New England,
filled with the tall masts of ships that had sailed to China
and to Spain,
to the West Indies and back.
Now there was only the salt smell of the sea
and the cry of gulls in an empty port.

Every day,
there were more and more of the king's soldiers
marching on Boston Common.
Or walking with a swagger
in their bright red coats
along the streets of our town.
Or cutting down our fences and our trees for their firewood.
King George wanted General Gage
to make sure that we kept his new laws
and that we paid our taxes to England.
Every penny.
My father said that by now there was one British soldier
for every five of us in Boston.
People called them "lobster backs" because of their coats.
Most of us didn't like General Gage's troops in our town.
Most of them didn't like us either.

But King George's laws hadn't closed
the South Writing School on West Street.
No one had told our schoolmaster,
Mr. Andrews,
to stay home and not teach.
So my brothers,
Colin and Ben,
and I still had to study our lessons each day:
first reading,
then writing,
then arithmetic and navigation.

One thing His Majesty King George couldn't stop
was the winter snow
in the colony of Massachusetts.

After days of hard frost and ice,
the snow fell for three nights in a row,
fine and thick.

Then, on my ninth birthday,
the gray clouds blew out to sea,
and the sun shone above the steeples of our town.

It was the best kind of New England day:
a day for coasting on Boston Common
for any boy or girl who had a sled.
And now I had my very own.
It was small
but it was mine,
made by my father's strong, steady hands,
with slick beef bones for runners
and a wood plank seat . . .
a present to me at breakfast
in a year of hard times.

That morning at school,
we practiced our handwriting
in our copybooks.
I had written the day's date five times for Mr. Andrews:

22 December, 1774

Then, just before noon,
I tucked my copybook, pen, and ink pot
under the back bench of our schoolroom.
I grabbed my wool coat from a high hook.
Other students at the South Writing School
tramped home through the snow
for hot bean porridge.
But not Colin or Ben or I.
We had brought our sleds to school.
Our sister, Kate, was waiting for us outside the school door
with three slabs of corn bread and apple jam.
Some girls were afraid to go to the Common
because of General Gage's troops.
But my sister loved to sled ride.

We had to hurry.
Mr. Andrews would expect all boys back for lessons
at two o'clock sharp.

We pulled our sleds along the icy ruts of West Street.
The December wind was cold,
and I was glad to be wearing
Kate's old mittens and Ben's patched leather boots.

We crossed to the Common,
a wide, hilly field with fine new snow
and a frame of blue sky.
We hurried on past the stark row of lime trees
that John Hancock had given as a gift to the town . . .

and past the town's Wishing Stone,
but we had no time to stop and wish
that King George would change his harsh laws.

For over a hundred years
the Common had belonged to *everyone* in Boston.
Now it was covered by the barracks of General Gage's troops.
And they were everywhere, these troops,
officers and soldiers, drummers and cooks.
Three thousand of them,
here on Boston Common,
setting up their tents,
carrying letters and orders,
polishing boots and bayonets,
drilling, marching.

Everywhere across the Common,
my brothers and Kate and I
heard the shouted orders of officers
and the constant *tramp-tramp* of British boots.

○   ○   ○

Our father had told us to listen
with our eyes and with our ears
every time we went to the Common.
"Look sharp but don't look like you're looking."
Every patriot who thought King George was wrong
helped out the Sons of Liberty* in his own small way.

○   ○   ○

Suddenly,
I stopped and pulled on Colin's sleeve.
Some of General Gage's soldiers had placed their tents
and their cooking fires
right in the middle of our sled runs.
They had broken the ice on the Common's ponds so no one
could skate.
And they had knocked down the snow forts
the town boys had worked yesterday to build.

* A group of local Boston patriots who opposed the actions of the British.
  They often met in secret to discuss plans for independence.

We were steaming mad,
all four of us.
This was *our* Common.
These were *our* ponds to skate on.
And there were no better hills to sled on anywhere in Boston.
It seemed as if the British troops had made it *their* Common.

Now there was no open run to sled on.
So instead, we walked among the barracks,
and listened with our eyes and with our ears.
Ben began to count new sheds and tents and horses.
Kate and I counted kegs of powder and barrels of fish.
Colin counted officers.

Kate and I saw General Gage.
He was right there in front of us,
almost close enough to touch.
He looked like a general,
and he stood like a general.

But he didn't look mean.
Not like a tyrant who would close our harbor.
Not like a bully for King George.
And not like an old woman,
as some Boston newspapers called him.
He had slate-blue eyes
and was speaking kindly to his soldiers
who were setting up a tent.
General Gage looked like a man who would listen,
a good man,
a man like my father.

If I could just speak to General Gage for a few minutes,
maybe he would help us.
Maybe he would let us sled on our Common.
But I was just a town boy.
General Gage was the royal governor.
I'd have to be as brave as the Boston patriots
who told the king of England that his taxes were not fair.

I held on to my sled tightly
and took a deep breath.
"Hurry," I whispered to Kate.
"Go find Colin and Ben.
We're going to talk to General Gage."

And so we did,
right there in the middle of the Common,
with British soldiers all about us.

I walked up to General Gage,
tugged hard on his scarlet sleeve,
and asked if he would hear a town boy's complaint.
Some of his officers glared at me sternly
and began to order us away.
But the tall general turned and held up his hand to still them.
Then he said,
"Let this boy have his words."

And so I talked.
And General Gage listened.

I told him that the Boston Common belonged to all of us,
not just his soldiers.
I told him his troops had knocked down our snow forts,
and ruined our ponds for skating,
and that they had built their cook fires
in the middle of the best sled runs.

Then,
with Colin and Ben and Kate right beside me,
I said: "And it's my birthday, sir,
and I wish to use my new sled on the steepest hill in our town.
But I can't, you see, because of your men.
And we have to be back at our school by two o'clock for our lessons."

General Gage crossed his arms
and looked out across the snowy Common.
His officers stood nearby with stony faces.
No one spoke a word.

Then the general put his hand on my shoulder.
He told me I had a fine sled
and asked who had made it.
"My father," I said proudly.

He leaned down to inspect the other sleds.
Then he stood up and said in a general's voice:
"I'm a father as well as a soldier for my king . . .
I have sons,
and daughters, too," he added, nodding at Kate.
"And I know my own children
would like to sled this hill if they were here.
But they're back in England in school."

Then General Gage asked me my name.
"Henry, sir," I said,
standing as tall as I could.
"Henry Price."

"Henry." The general nodded.
"That's a good name, indeed."
He shook my hand, man to man.
"My oldest son is named Henry."

"I'm the youngest in our house," I said.

"You may be the youngest," said General Gage,
"but you have the courage of a good soldier
as well as the spunk of your local rebels."
He turned swiftly on his heel
to one of his officers.

"Instruct all troops
that they are to allow the town children
to sled where they wish.
And keep the ice unbroken in one of those ponds.
Tell the men they are to clear a good run.
And be quick about it.
It's my young friend's birthday,
and he needs to try out a new sled before two o'clock this day."

I'll never forget the first time I came down that hill
on a sled I could call my own:
down, down, down
the snowy path beneath my runners,
the tents and barrels blurring past,
the red coats of soldiers rushing past,
the wind on my face and in my eyes,
faster, faster,
over bumps and more bumps,
straight through the sprawling camp of British troops
till I reached the bottom of the Common,

then slower,
slower,
slow,
till I slid to a stop,
never wanting that ride to end.

Again and again,
my brothers and my sister and I
sledded down the best hill in Boston
and then dragged our sleds to the top,
until it was time to hurry back
to the South Writing School
for Mr. Andrews's afternoon lessons.

And from December 22 on,
Colin and Ben and Kate and I had other days
of good sledding on the Common.
And skating, too.
Because General Thomas Gage was a man of his word.

Spring came,
and in April of 1775,
the War for Independence began
after General Gage ordered his troops to Lexington and Concord.
Our new country was at war,
and the lobster backs in our town
would soon be under seige.
The next October, the good folk of Boston
were glad when King George sent orders
for his top general to return to England.
Thomas Gage was the last royal governor
of a colony that wanted to choose its own.

On the night that his ship left Boston Harbor
and set sail for England,
I stood on Long Wharf with my brothers and Kate.
We were Americans now,
my family and I.
We were Boston patriots hoping to win a war against a king.
But we'd never forget the tall British general
that we'd met on my birthday.
General Gage had given us back
a pond and our sled runs on Boston Common
because he had children of his own.
Indeed, he was a good man.

AUTHOR'S NOTES

○

Boston Common

In 1634, the town of Boston purchased land for the purpose of creating a common. Taxes were levied to pay for this land. Cows grazed on the large acreage of pasture, criminals were hanged there, and the local militia marched and drilled. During colonial times in the eighteenth century, the Boston Common had a very high hill that was used for sledding.

From September of 1768 until the British evacuated Boston on March 17, 1776, regiments of King George III's soldiers were continually encamped on the Boston Common. Local folklore has stated that in the winter of 1775–76, some boys of Boston confronted a British general, supposedly General Gage, and demanded that his soldiers stop destroying their local sled runs. Since Thomas Gage was recalled to England in October of 1775 and was not present in Boston during the winter of 1775–76, I decided to have this story take place in December of 1774. Diaries, newspapers, and letters from that year mention cold weather and snow during the week before Christmas. I have used original street names and the South Writing School from old Boston maps. Henry, Colin, Ben, and Kate Price, as written about in this story, are fictitious characters.

General Thomas Gage

Thomas Gage was born in 1721. There is no official record of his birth. It is not known where he was born but he lived in the county of Gloucestershire, England, during his childhood. At the age of eight, he was enrolled at Westminster School in London and attended this school for eight years. Later, his own sons would attend Westminster.

Thomas Gage was an honest and mild-mannered general, well-liked by the men who served under him. He was often sympathetic to the hardships endured by the common British soldier. General Gage was married to an American, Margaret Kemble, of New Jersey, and was the father of six sons and five daughters. Some of his children did not survive childhood.

After he was recalled to England from America in 1775, Thomas Gage never served as a military commander again. He died on April 2, 1787, and is buried in the family crypt at St. Peter's Church in Firle, England, near his ancestral home, Firle Place. No inscription marks his tomb. Most of Thomas Gage's official correspondence is now kept in a rare manuscript collection at the William L. Clements Library at the University of Michigan in Ann Arbor.

for Margaret McElderry
— L.B.

To my mother
— R.A.P.

The author would like to thank John Harriman and
Brian Dunnigan at the William L. Clements Library
(University of Michigan, Ann Arbor), Peter Stark,
Cat Smith, M. K. Kroeger, and the curators of Firle
Place, Lewes, England, for their help in researching
sledding, Boston Common, and Thomas Gage.

Warm thanks also to Michael Foreman, George Ella
Lyon, Johanna Hurwitz, Florence Heide, Pat Giff,
Trish Marx, Karen Riskin, Emma Dryden, Ann Bobco,
and my husband, Pete, for their belief in this book.